D1459441

The Sleepover Club

Have you been invited to all these sleepovers?

Sleepover Girls on the Catwalk

by Sue Mongredien

Collins

An Imprint of HarperCollins*Publishers*

For Martin Powell – who loves clothes

The Sleepover Club ® is a
registered trademark of HarperCollins*Publishers* Ltd

First published in Great Britain by Collins in 1999
Collins is an imprint of HarperCollins*Publishers* Ltd
77-85 Fulham Palace Road, Hammersmith,
London, W6 8JB

The HarperCollins website address is
www.**fire**and**water**.com

1 3 5 7 9 8 6 4 2

Text copyright © Sue Mongredien 1999

Original series characters, plotlines
and settings © Rose Impey 1997

ISBN 0 00675449-X

The author asserts the moral right to
be identified as the author of the work.

Printed and bound in Great Britain by
Caledonian International Book Manufacturing Ltd,
Glasgow G64

Conditions of Sale
This book is sold subject to the condition
that it shall not, by way of trade or otherwise,
be lent, re-sold, hired out or otherwise circulated
without the publisher's prior consent in any form,
binding or cover other than that in which it is
published and without a similar condition
including this condition being imposed
on the subsequent purchaser.

Sleepover Kit List

1. Sleeping bag
2. Pillow
3. Pyjamas or a nightdress
4. Slippers
5. Toothbrush, toothpaste, soap etc
6. Towel
7. Teddy
8. A creepy story
9. Food for a midnight feast:
   chocolate, crisps, sweets, biscuits.
   In fact anything you like to eat.
10. Torch
11. Hairbrush
12. Hair things like a bobble or hairband,
    if you need them
13. Clean knickers and socks
14. Change of clothes for the next day
15. Sleepover diary and membership card

CHAPTER ONE

Hello, it's me again – that's Felicity Diana Sidebotham if you didn't know. You can call me Fliss, though – everyone else does. Some of the boys in our class sometimes call me other things – usually stupid versions of my surname, but we won't go into that now.

Anyway, everyone thought I'd done such a good job writing about when we were detectives, I decided to tell you about this story too. In case you don't know, I'd better explain about the Sleepover Club, otherwise you might not want to finish the story – and believe me, it's a good one, so you should.

Let me start at the beginning. We're the Sleepover Club – me, Frankie, Kenny, Lyndz and Rosie. Once a week we sleep over at each other's houses which is always brill – apart from when Kenny tries to scare me with her horrible ghost stories, that is.

I'm Fliss, like I said, and the oldest of the club – in fact I'm the oldest in our class at school. I'm quite tall so sometimes people think I'm even older. People have told me I'm pretty too, but that's not really something I like to go on about. Hopefully I'll take after my mum though. She used to be a model, you know!

If you haven't met the others, I'll give you a quick catch-up on them. Frankie and Kenny are the maddest ones of the club – and the loudest too, my mum says. Frankie is always having these wild ideas that we usually end up getting tangled up in somehow – and which end up going wrong most of the time. Life's never boring when you're with Frankie! Just so you'll recognise her, Frankie's tall and quite skinny. She's always wearing something a bit weird like silver nail varnish, or fluffy slippers, or – you know. The sort of thing my mum would go bonkers about if I came home wearing!

Kenny – real name Laura McKenzie, although don't ever call her that or she'll karate-chop you – is about as different from me as you can get, but I still like her (most of the time…). First of all, she's mad about sport – especially boring old Leicester City Football Club, which she just lurves – and she's always trying to get us to run about and get all hot and sweaty playing some stoo-pid game or other.

I don't mind netball or proper games like that (I'm in the netball first team at school, if you didn't know) but some of Kenny's games get really reeeeeally wild, with loads of wrestling around on the ground and getting covered in mud! So if she ever asks you if you want a game of McKenzie Football with her – I seriously advise you to say no, quick!

Second, she's got this real thing about blood and guts. Ugh!! Kenny can make me feel sick sometimes, talking about bodies and all the yucky things inside them. She wants to be a doctor so she can poke about with people's intestines all day, she says. I just can't think of anything more gross though, getting your hands covered in bits of people's bodies and... Yee-uck, pass me the bucket, per-lease!

Ooh, excuse me.

Just came over all funny. I hate the sight of blood and even *thinking* about it... Let's change the subject.

Kenny's a good friend though, because she's the type of person who'll stick up for you in a flash if you're ever getting picked on or anything. Like last week, she helped me out when I had a bit of a bust-up with the M&Ms. Oh – you might not know our big enemies at school, the M&Ms (also known as Emma Hughes and Emily Berryman – ugh! ugh! ugh!!!! VILE!) – but I bet there's people like them in your class at school. They're always being mean and trying to play tricks on us – you know the sort. Pigs in school uniform, that's what Frankie calls them.

You see, last week they started teasing me about Ryan Scott, this boy in our class. I mean, I can't help it if he likes me, can I? But they just went on and on about it, thinking they were dead funny by saying stupid rhymes, like: *"Felicity and Ryan, sitting in a tree, K-I-S-S-I-N-G!"* and giggling whenever I said anything, or calling me "Mrs Scott" across the classroom, and – oh, you know the sort of thing.

Anyway, I was getting a bit sick of it but I was also feeling reeeeeeally embarrassed after a while – because Ryan could hear all of it too. It was awful!

But suddenly, I heard Kenny's voice, loud and clear as always.

"Oh, because it's such a shame that no boys will ever fancy *you* two – Emma with that massive conk sticking out of her face, and Emily with her mouth like a cat's bum!"

Kenny's voice is so loud that I think the whole classroom heard. There was this moment of silence – like everyone in the room gasping at once – and then we all just burst out laughing. I mean, *everyone*. Even Mrs Weaver, our teacher, sort of spluttered a bit. You could see her trying not to smile too. It was awesome! Kenny gave me this dead cheeky wink, and the M&Ms shut up for the rest of the day.

Anyway. That's Kenny for you.

Then there's Lyndz. What can I tell you about her? She's mad about animals, especially horses and dogs. I'm a bit scared of her dog, Buster, if you must know. I don't trust him because he sometimes jumps up at you and barks really loudly. But Buster's just as barmy about Lyndz as she is about him, so if we're round at her house, Buster's usually with us – worse luck (don't tell Lyndz I said that!).

As well as Buster and the three cats, Lyndz also has four – yes, FOUR! – brothers, which I reckon must be a nightmare. One brother's bad enough for me, thanks! Sometimes boys are so stupid and annoying – girls are much better, I think. My little brother Callum is nice sometimes but most of the time I think he's a big pain in the you-know-what. I don't know how Lyndz puts up with it.

There's only one boy who I think is remotely OK, and that's Ryan Scott at school. I'm not going to go on about him though, especially after all the stick I had from those horrible M&Ms, and also because the others will all just take the mickey out of me too. They're just jealous 'cos he likes me best, I reckon. He's nice anyway, you've got my word for it. And good-looking. And he wears nice clothes. But that's enough about him for now!

Last is Rosie who's the newest member of the club. Well, I say 'new' but it feels like she's been hanging around with us for ages and ages now. Rosie's nice, when she's not being grumpy. You'll like her.

Right, come on, let's go and see if Mum's finished vacuuming upstairs. I want to show you my bedroom, but we won't be able to have a good old chin-wag if she's in there. Hang on... oh, ace, the coast's clear. She's gone to clean Callum's room, which will take her the rest of the day I should think! Now we can get cosy and I can tell you all about the day us five went on the catwalk. Seriously!

Oh – but would you mind taking your shoes off first? That rug cost a fortune, you know. That's better. Thanks.

Anyway, on with the story. It all started with my brilliant idea at Brownies. No, wait, I suppose it started before that. Oh, help! This is more difficult than you think!

Do you know what? I think I'm going to start a new chapter. It feels a bit late in this one to launch into the main story. I promise I'll get on with it in Chapter Two. Honest!

CHAPTER TWO

I suppose it started just *before* Brownies, actually. The others had come round for tea at my house and we'd all got into our uniforms together in my bedroom and were just messing about a bit before Andy drove us there – oh, whoops, forgot to mention Andy. He's my step-dad – well, he and my mum aren't actually married, but I call him my step-dad anyway. He's OK, I suppose.

We had about an hour before we had to go, so I started showing the others my new clothes for our family holiday. If you didn't know, I *love* clothes. I've got an awesome collection. Don't get me started though, or I'll be showing you my new jeans Mum bought me from Gap last Saturday...

The others aren't really bothered about fashion – not like me. Like I said, Frankie wears a lot of weird things that I wouldn't be seen dead in, Kenny's always in her smelly old football top, Lyndz likes mucking about in her jodhpurs or jeans, and Rosie – well, I don't think Rosie's mum can afford many new clothes for Rosie, to be honest. Don't say I told you, though.

So when I announced that I was going to show them what me and Mum had bought in Cuddington the weekend before, they all started groaning and pulling faces.

"Bo-ring," Kenny moaned. "A pair of trousers is a pair of trousers, if you ask me."

"Well done, Kenny," Rosie said sarcastically. "And there was me thinking a pair of trousers was a skirt!"

"Where are you off to this year then, Fliss?" Frankie asked me quickly before a scrap broke out.

"Majorca," I said. "I told you before, remember? I'll just show you this sun-dress I've got. It's gorgeous! It's got spaghetti straps and everything!"

"What, so you can eat them if you get peckish?" Kenny said, winking at Frankie.

I ignored that remark. "Look!" I said, pulling it out from the wardrobe.

"Ooh, it *is* nice," said Lyndz. "Dead summery."

Thank goodness! Someone taking an interest at last! "And I've got these shorts…" I said, showing them some new denim cut-offs.

"You want to take those back, Fliss, they're fraying at the bottom!" said Frankie, all seriously.

"They're meant to be like that!" I said. "Honestly, Frankie, you—"

But Frankie and Kenny had collapsed in giggles and were rolling around on my bed, gurgling with laughter.

"I think she was joking, Fliss," said Lyndz.

"Oh," I said, feeling a bit silly. "Right.

Anyway, I've got these trousers too, for the evenings when it's a bit cooler…"

"Let's see them properly, then," Rosie said. "Show us what they look like on *you*, not the hangers!"

"Yeah, if you're gonna bore us with your clothes, you might as well go the whole hog!" Kenny said. "*Joking*, Fliss!" she added before I could strangle her.

"Shall I put them on, then?" I said, hoping Rosie hadn't just been joking too.

"Yeah, do it!" said Lyndz.

"Shall we *all* do it?" I said suddenly. I didn't want them thinking I was selfish or anything. "Shall we all try my holiday clothes on for a giggle?"

"What, like a fashion show?" Frankie said, sitting up on the bed. She'd stopped snorting with laughter by then, thank goodness.

"Yes," I said. "*Exactly* like a fashion show!"

It was quite funny, seeing the others all getting dressed up for a change. The sight of Kenny in my new white mini-skirt and her own scruffy old trainers was *sooo* hysterical. You should have seen her!

"What's the big joke?" she growled crossly, as we all burst out laughing at the same time.

"Ooh, darling, you look so... *feminine!*" Frankie said. "Go on, try on this cropped top with it – let's see your belly button!"

"Ugh, no chance!" Kenny said. "I've decided, I don't suit skirts – this one's coming off straightaway!"

"Careful, Kenny, don't crease it," I said anxiously, watching her wrenching it off. You could tell she wasn't used to wearing nice things. "Why don't you try these velvet trousers instead?"

As for me, of course I was totally into the whole thing. I started being silly to make them all laugh – wiggling my bum and tossing my hair about.

"Ooh, Fliss the supermodel!" giggled Lyndz. "Go, girl, flash us a smile!"

"Strut your stuff, babe!" Frankie yelled as I pranced up and down the bedroom.

"More like Babe the pig, if you ask me," came a voice from outside the room.

Guess who? I marched over and pulled the door open. You got it – Callum, the brat brother.

"Babe the pig, Babe the pig!" he chanted at me, sticking his tongue out. He is such a...

"Get him!" Kenny shouted, and chucked one of my teddies at him.

"Babe the pig, Fliss looks like Babe the pig," he shouted over his shoulder, running off down the stairs. "Oink! Oink!"

"It's war!" I yelled fiercely. "Come here, you pain!"

We all piled down to the living room, and were just about to *kill* him – death by suffocation from Kenny's stinky trainers – when unfortunately Mum put her head round the door.

"What on earth do you think you're doing?" she shouted. "Girls, leave Callum alone. And Callum, stop climbing on the sofa. If you've left any marks on it, you're in trouble!"

Callum scuttled off, and the five of us stood there panting, all wearing different outfits. Mum wasn't impressed.

"Felicity, those clothes are for your holiday, not to go charging around the house in!" she said in this awful tight little voice. "Now, all of you – get back into your Brownie uniforms, quick! It's almost time to go!"

When Mum gets that cross note in her voice, you kind of do what she says, and fast – unless you enjoy serious amounts of getting told off, that is.

We pelted back upstairs and put our Brownie uniforms on again.

"Typical of that nerd to interrupt," I grumbled, fastening my belt. "I was enjoying that."

"Yeah, we could tell," Frankie said.

"I wouldn't mind being a model," I told them. "It must be brilliant, having everyone make a fuss of you all day, and wearing lots of gorgeous, expensive clothes in the fashion-shoots."

"I can't think of anything more dull," Kenny said in a muffled voice, as she pulled her Brownie dress over her head.

"It'd be OK having lots of wicked make-up

on, and having hair stylists doing loads of mad things with your hair, I suppose," Frankie said thoughtfully.

"Wedding dresses would be good…" I said.

"What, with Ryan Scott modelling the groom's outfit?" Rosie said, elbowing me in the ribs. "I get it!"

The others started making kissy noises and saying "Oh, *Ryyyan*!" in silly voices, and I felt myself going a bit red.

"Well, he is good-looking enough to be a model," I protested. I mean, he really is!!

"Oooh, Fliss, got it all planned, have you?" Lyndz said, giggling.

"Here comes the bride, all fat and wide!" Kenny sang. Well, I say "sang" but Kenny's got one of the worst singing voices I've ever heard.

"I am *not* all fat and wide!" I said crossly, sticking my tongue out at her. "I'm the perfect size for my age, the doctor told my mum, so there!"

"Ooh, get you!" Frankie said. "Ooh, I so wish *I* could be as perfect as Fliss!"

"Girls! Time to go!" Andy shouted up the

stairs. Just as well – I was getting a bit sick of this conversation.

"Go on, model, lead the way," Rosie said.

"Go for it, gorgeous," Frankie added.

I ignored them, and swished out of the room, nose in the air. Still… it had got me thinking.

It had got me thinking that suddenly I really *reeeeally* wanted to be a model!

CHAPTER THREE

I like Brownies. I even like the uniform, even
though brown's my worst colour by miles. We
always have good fun, and it's brilliant getting
badges. Kenny gets all the sporty ones, and
Frankie and Rosie like the arty-farty ones, but
I prefer getting the badges where you have to
use your brain a bit more, like Safety in the
Home, which is very useful. I think it's sensible
to know about things like that. I've got more
badges than anyone in my Six, actually.

This week, I was wondering what we were
going to do next. Our whole pack had just
gone for the First Aid badge, and we'd all

passed it the week before. It was good, apart from when they talked about blood and things like that, which made me feel a bit sick. Surprise, surprise, that was gore-monster Kenny's favourite bit...

Anyway, like I was saying, I was kind of wondering what Brown Owl was going to get us doing next. Usually we do lots of things in our Sixes or play games, all together. But there's always something that the pack work on as a group – often a badge we're all doing, or our Brownie Highway stuff.

Brown Owl had us sitting in a ring as usual, and we all paid our subs into the toadstool in the middle, and said the Brownie promise. Then Brown Owl stood up in the middle and looked serious.

"Tonight, I want us to think about holidays," she said. "Obviously you're all off school at the moment for the summer holidays, and some of the luckier Brownies may be going away on holiday soon, or have already been. What does holiday time mean to you?"

"Going abroad and getting a good tan!" I said

straightaway. I only meant to mutter it to myself because I'm not normally the sort to speak up in front of the whole Brownie pack like that. Frankie and Kenny are usually much louder than me, but because I'd been thinking about it, it just kind of burst out of me, louder than I meant it to.

"Thank you, Felicity. Hands up, please," Brown Owl said. "Rosie?"

"No school!"

Everyone started shouting things out.

"Going to the beach!"

"Going to see my cousins!"

"Going to Disneyworld in Florida!" Emma Hughes yelled out, just so everyone could hear. *Such* a show-off.

"Staying up late!"

"Good, good," said Brown Owl. "So we all enjoy holidays, don't we?"

"Yeeeah!" everyone shouted.

"Right," Brown Owl said. "Well, now I want us to think about the people who aren't as lucky as you lot – who can't go abroad, or to the beach – who might not have any family to go with, even if they could."

We'd all gone quiet, wondering what was coming next.

"I'm talking about the old people's home in town," Brown Owl told us. "Some of the people there never get to leave Cuddington. They're old, and some of them get very lonely. I want you to think about how it must feel to be an old lady, living in a home like that."

GRIM!!! I couldn't help shuddering as Brown Owl said that. What an awful thought! Being wrinkly and ancient and stuck inside all the time. I couldn't think of anything more depressing.

"That's why I've decided that our Brownie pack is going to give them a bit of a treat," Brown Owl said with a big smile. "We're going to put on a show for them at the end of this month – and you Brownies are going to decide just what sort of a show we're going to do!"

"How about working out some dance routines?" Emily suggested loudly. Just because she reckoned she was an ace dancer. Ugh, no thanks – who'd want to be bossed around by one of the Gruesome Twosome? Not likely!

"Magic tricks!" Frankie shouted, trying to drown her out.

"*A fashion show!*" I blurted out. It was a brilliant idea, I knew it!!! *And I could be the star model!!*

"A gymnastics display!" Kenny shouted out straight afterwards. I should have known *she* wouldn't be keen on my idea!

It was getting a bit chaotic – everyone was shouting things out at once. In the end, Brown Owl blew on her whistle – *screeeee!* – and the hall fell silent.

"Thank you!" she said. "Well, I'm glad you've got lots of ideas between you – that's an excellent start. It's probably best if we put on a few different acts – rather like a talent show. So, first things first, let's sort out which Six is going to do what."

"We're doing a fashion show," I told my Six. After all, I was a Sixer so I was the boss.

"That's not fair," Kelly Morgan, my Seconder said. "Me and Jacinta play recorder – we want to do a song, don't we?"

"Yeah," said Jacinta.

"Well... well, you can't," I said. Now I had my sights set on a fashion show, I was desperate to do it.

"Why not?" Kelly answered.

"Because... because I said so!" I told them, feeling my face go a bit hot. I don't like arguments, but couldn't bear the thought of losing my fashion show.

All round the hall, similar conversations were going on. Not one Six could decide what to do without having a row over it.

I saw Snowy Owl – who's my Aunty Jill actually – go over and whisper something to Brown Owl.

Then Kelly spoke up again. "Excuse me, Brown Owl, but there's about five of us that are in the school band and play instruments – can't we work out a song together? Do we have to stay in Sixes?"

I felt myself going red. Oh no, my Seconder didn't want to be in my group! How embarrassing was that?

29

"And us dancers would like to put together a dance routine," Emily said smugly. "Not all of us want to mess around with magic tricks!" She was in Frankie's Six, and Frankie glared at her so fiercely that anyone weedier than Emily might have passed out from the force of it. Unfortunately, Emily was used to Frankie's glares and ignored it.

Brown Owl and Snowy Owl exchanged looks. Then Brown Owl clapped her hands. "All right, girls," she said. "Usually I'd want you to work in Sixes, but this time, as your talents are spread around the Brownie pack, it might make sense if you choose your groups according to what you're good at. Let's have a singing group, a dancing group, a group that wants to put on a play – get together in groups of five or six, and work it for yourselves. I'll give you five minutes to come up with some ideas."

YIPPEEEEE!! Of course, us Sleepovers made a beeline for each other.

"That's good!" I said. "Now we can do my fashion show, can't we – oh, can we? Please?"

"Gymnastics!" Kenny said hotly, folding her arms across her chest. "I don't want to prance around in stoo-pid outfits for the old grannies!"

"Well, you could model your football kit, then," I told her. "If you really have to. Go on, Kenny." I was practically begging her.

"You could even do a few gymnastic moves as part of your bit," Lyndz suggested.

"It's either that or join the other gymnastics lot, Kenny," I told her warningly. "And look who's in charge of *that* group!"

We looked over, and Kenny groaned. Emma Hughes, who'd done her BAGA One, was bossing her group about in the corner. "Any more for gymnastics?" she called across the hall.

"No, thanks," Kenny said, with feeling.

"How come Fliss gets to decide?" Frankie said. "Why don't we do a magic show? I know loads of tricks my dad's taught me..."

"I said it first!" I told her. "*And* Snowy Owl's my aunt." I knew it was a bit of a feeble argument but it was the best I could think of.

31

"So what?" Frankie said.

"It might be a laugh, Frankie," Lyndz said. "We could each make our own costumes to model! I'm going to be a cow-girl – or maybe a jockey!"

We all groaned. Lyndz is so nuts about animals, I reckon she's going to turn into one some day.

"Why not just go for it, and dress up as a horse?" Rosie said, laughing.

"I could do, couldn't I?" Lyndz started getting carried away, making horse noises. "Ne-e-eigh!"

Kenny suddenly jumped on her back. "Giddy up, horsey!" she yelled.

Rosie jumped on Frankie's back and Frankie staggered, nearly falling over in shock. "We'll race you two!" Rosie called to Kenny. "Go, horsey, go!"

Just then, Brown Owl blew her whistle – and the two horses crashed into each other, with everyone falling off in a heap.

"Girls!" she called to us. "Have you decided what you're going to do?"

"Yes," I said quickly, while the others were picking themselves up. "We've decided to do a fashion show!"

CHAPTER FOUR

So that was that. Brown Owl wrote it down on her list, and the others had to go along with it. ACE!!!!

I couldn't quite believe it. Are you surprised at *me*, Fliss, bossing the others around like that? I know, I was a bit too. Normally Frankie or Kenny make all the decisions – just 'cos they're the loudest, I suppose. But fair's fair, like Mum always says. Kenny shot me a look that said she wasn't happy about it, and I tried to smile back. I think I just looked nervous, though.

"Right, girls," Brown Owl said when every

group had told her what they were going to do. "I want you to stay in your groups and make a plan of action. Snowy Owl will come round with some paper and pencils. We're going to have the show on August 14th, so that gives you a couple of weeks to work out what you're doing, then rehearse it – and then rehearse some more!"

Out of the corner of my eye I could see Kenny scowling, and I tried to ignore her. She'd come round to my brilliant idea eventually – at least I hoped she would! I crossed my fingers, suddenly feeling worried that I'd gone too far. Like I said, sticking my neck out just wasn't like me. But all models had to start somewhere, didn't they? And I planned to start right here, right now.

"Aren't you going to be on holiday then, Fliss?" Kenny suddenly asked, elbowing me in the ribs. I could see a glimmer of hope shining in her eyes at the thought of getting out of my idea.

"Week after," I whispered back, and her face fell again.

"Oh."

"We've got…" Brown Owl counted down the list she'd made – "six groups here, so if each group has roughly a ten-minute slot each, that makes the show an hour long. I can't wait to see what you're going to come up with – it sounds like we're going to put together a wonderful show between us!"

I suddenly had a vision of myself looking dead glamorous walking down the catwalk in a fabulous outfit and everyone gasping in amazement at how good I looked. Flash-bulbs would be popping, journalists scribbling down details of my outfit, designers all trying to book me for their next shows… it was just a dream come true.

"Snowy Owl and I will be coming round to give you any help you might need but other than that – it's down to you, girls!"

An excited babble broke out as everyone started discussing what they were going to do for the show.

"Look at Fliss, you lot," Frankie said in a loud kind of whisper. "She's got that mad glint in her eye! Supermodel here I come, she's thinking!"

"I have not got a mad glint!" I said indignantly.

"How has this happened?" Kenny was groaning. "How have I got myself into this? I hate clothes!"

"Oh, I dunno," said Rosie. "I thought you looked good in that mini-skirt, Kenz. Very… *you*."

"Mmm, darling!" Lyndz simpered, trying not to crack up as Kenny's face looked more and more thunderous.

"Let's decide what we're all going to wear," I said, grabbing a pencil and some paper. Someone had to take charge of this lot!

"Well, I'm not wearing a skirt," said Kenny. "So you two can shut up!" She was practically growling the words out.

"Frankie, what are you going to wear?" I said, trying not to giggle at Kenny's murderous expression.

"I think I'm going to make something," she answered mysteriously. You could almost hear her brain ticking away as she hatched some plot or other. You know what Frankie's like with her mad ideas!

"Make what?" Lyndz said. "A cup of tea for the oldies in the interval?"

"Some chocolate brownies?" Rosie said. "Mmm, yummo!"

"An outfit, you durr-brains," Frankie said, rolling her eyes right back into her head. Then she paused – you could see the idea taking shape in her head. "Maybe a magician's outfit, so I can do some magic tricks after all…"

"Frankie, models don't usually do magic tricks on the catwalk," I reminded her, trying to be patient. Honestly, they were my best friends but I was starting to think they had no *idea*!

"If Kenny can wear her footy kit and do gymnastics, I think I can do a few magic tricks!" she retorted sharply.

Uh-oh. I'd just remembered Frankie didn't like being bossed around by anyone.

"I've got it!" Frankie then said suddenly. "I'm going to make a spaceman outfit!"

"That's a good idea," Lyndz said. "Spaceman by name, spaceman by nature!"

It *was* quite a good idea, actually. One of Frankie's nicknames is Spaceman because she's absolutely mad about silver things. Mmm, I know what you're thinking – *weird* – but that's Frankie's taste for you. One day, ages ago, she'd turned up at Kenny's house wearing this silver catsuit thing her mum had found in a charity shop with great big clodhopping boots, and Kenny just gave her one look and said, "Been to the moon again, Frankie?" We all cracked up and started teasing her about being from outer space, and the name just stuck.

Even Kenny was looking a bit more interested now. "How are you going to make a spaceman costume?" she asked. "Silver foil round your clothes and a crash helmet, or what?"

"Or you could just go futuristic – like something from the next century!" Rosie suggested.

Frankie gave her a look. "It's 1999, Rosie –

next century is next *year*," she reminded her. "But I know what you mean, I could go for the full-on space babe thing, couldn't I – silver dreads, laser guns, wild make-up…"

"Why not go the whole hog and be an alien?" Kenny said. "*Bleeeeurgh!!*"

We all jumped at Kenny's horrible alien noise, especially Lyndz, who Kenny'd grabbed. But that set Lyndz off giggling and next thing we knew – you guessed it – she got the hiccups.

Lyndz is a nightmare for uncontrollable hiccups. I seriously think she's got something wrong with her insides. Any excuse and she'll let rip with the loudest, squeakiest and most high-pitched noises you've ever heard.

"Oh, no," she gasped. "I've got the… hic!… hiccups again!"

This was Frankie's cue to leap on her and start tickling her, to try and shock her into stopping.

"It was your – aargh! – alien that did it, Kenz!" Lyndz moaned, as she struggled with Frankie.

Just then there was a familiar sound – *screeeeee!* – as Brown Owl blew her whistle to quiet everyone down.

"Settle down, girls," she called, clapping her hands.

Lyndz immediately clamped her lips tight shut, so no hiccups could escape. Lyndz gets embarrassed easily, and if she let out a massive hiccup in the middle of Brown Owl talking, I knew she'd be *reeeeeaally* gutted.

"It sounds like there are some great ideas out there," Brown Owl was saying, "and in order to spur you on just that little bit more, Snowy Owl and I are going to give a little prize to the group of Brownies who put on the best act."

"What's the prize?" Emma shouted out. Like she reckoned *she'd* win, of course.

Brown Owl smiled as every single Brownie sat up in interest. "We haven't quite decided, but it'll probably be something like a trip to the new leisure centre in Oakworth – you know, the one with the wave machine and all the big slides into the pool for the

41

winning group."

"Coo-ell!" whispered Kenny, eyes nearly popping out of her head. "That would be *awesome!*"

Kenny is sports mad, remember. And when I say mad, I mean *lost the plot.* I could tell she was having to restrain herself from bouncing up and down in excitement, as Brown Owl told us more about the prize. Bonus! It sounded good – *and* now it meant that I had Kenny all fired up about making it a wicked show and trying to win.

And there was me thinking that I was going to have a totally no-way situation on my hands!

Well, one quick game of Bulldog and that was the end of Brownies. Us Sleepover Clubbers were well excited about the show now! The competition was on!

Kenny grabbed my arm on the way out.

"We've got to win this, Fliss," she said, eyes sparkling. "I want to get this prize! Emergency sleepover needed to plan, plan and plan!"

"Agreed," I said importantly. "How about my house, Saturday night?"

"Cool," said Frankie. "And everyone has to bring at least ten brilliant ideas, or else!"

"And lots of… hic!… scrummy food!" said Lyndz. "Chocolate's good for the brain, after all!"

"Who told you that?" laughed Rosie.

"I made it up," Lyndz confessed. "But I'm sure it's good for *my* brain!"

Just as we were about to leave the hall, though, the M&Ms came up to us.

"Think you're going to win with your stupid little fashion show then, do you?" Emma sneered. "You must be joking!"

"You need talent to win a talent show," Emily agreed, folding her arms across her chest smugly. "And let's face it – you lot wouldn't know talent if it hit you in the face!"

"You'd know my fist if it hit you in the face!" Kenny growled, making a lunge for Emily. Emily dodged her neatly, and then the pair of them ran off.

"Break a leg, darling!" Emma shouted in a

stupid voice, and then they collapsed in giggles.

"They are so *unfunny*!" Frankie said angrily.

"They're such saddos!" Rosie said scornfully. "Like we're really going to care what *they* think!"

"Just wait, you M&Ms," Kenny said through gritted teeth. "They're going to get such a shock when we win! I can't wait to wipe the smug looks off their faces!"

Frankie's mum was waiting outside to take us home. Our mums and dads take it in turns to drop us off places, although I prefer our car to all the others. Lyndz's car smells all doggy from mad Buster, and Frankie's parents are always blasting out opera from the car stereo which gives me a headache.

That night though, Frankie sat in the front seat and switched the music off, to her mum's surprise. "We need some peace and quiet, Mum," she said solemnly. "We've got serious brain-work to do!"

"Not to mention serious prize-winning!" Kenny said. "Get your brainy heads on, all of you. I want to win this thing – even if it does mean dressing up in stoo-pid clothes! We're gonna beat those M&Ms if it's the last thing we do!!"

CHAPTER FIVE

I could hardly sleep that night, my brain was going so bonkers. I know it sounds daft – and don't you dare tell the others – but I'd always had this secret thing about being a model, so I was just dead, dead excited about our fashion show. And what was I going to wear?!!!

We were going to meet up again on Saturday for lunch and a sleepover at mine, so I had all of Friday to kill. Luckily it was the summer holidays so there was no school, but unfortunately Mum dragged me off round the supermarket and then roped me in to help clean the house.

"If you've invited your friends to come round again, the least you can do is help me tidy up for them," she said. Don't you just hate it when parents say things like that?

Saturday finally arrived, and Kenny turned up grinning from ear to ear.

"Guess who I've just bumped into?" she said. By the way she was beaming, I thought it must be some yucky footballer or something, but she shook her head wildly when I suggested it.

"Better," she said. "The M&Ms!"

"Ugh," said Frankie. "Worse, don't you mean? *The* worst!"

"Poor you," Lyndz agreed.

"So what did you say to those old poo-bags?" Frankie asked with a scowl.

"I asked who was going to win out of their two groups," Kenny told us. "Just to stir up an argument, you know!"

For the first time in simply ages, the M&Ms were going to be split up for the show – Emily was doing her stupid dancing ("An elephant with an itchy bum" was how Kenny had once described Emily's dancing) and Emma was doing a gymnastics display. It was strange, the two of them competing against each other when usually they were such a team.

"Well, Emma *is* brilliant at gymnastics, but I think the dancers will win, actually," Emily had said with her usual smug grin.

Emma's face was a Kodak moment, according to Kenny.

"And what do you think, Ems?" Kenny had then asked wickedly.

"Well, I know Emily's a good dancer, but I think gymnastics is slightly more skilful, actually," Emma said haughtily.

Ouch! If looks could kill, Emma would apparently have carked it there and then!

"Most excellent," Kenny said happily to us. "Nobble the opposition, that's what I like to do! I could hear them arguing about it all the way down the street! We're going to blow 'em off stage!"

"I wish we really could," said Frankie. "Blow them away, I mean. Wouldn't the world be a lovelier place with no M&Ms to bug us?"

48

"What a heavenly thought," sighed Lyndz. "If only!"

"Right, down to business!" I announced as soon as lunch was over. We all raced out into the garden. "What's everyone going to wear?"

"I'm going to be a cowboy!" Lyndz said straightaway.

"Really?" I asked, trying not to sound too disappointed. I mean, it was hardly *Vogue*, was it?

"Really," Lyndz said, turning just the tiniest bit pink as everyone looked at her. "You know that wicked cowboy hat in my dressing-up box? I'm going to wear that and my jodhpurs and my riding boots and..."

Frankie groaned loudly. "Trust old Pet Rescue Lyndz to find a way to wear her jodhpurs on the catwalk!"

I have to say, I agreed with Frankie. Lyndz loves animals – sometimes I think she loves them more than people. In fact, come to think of it, it was a bit of a miracle that she'd made it over to my house on a Saturday afternoon at all, when she'd usually have been horse riding. If there was any chance Lyndz could wear her beloved jods, then she'd do it!

"Hey Lyndz, why don't you dress up as Rolf Harris and do the Animal Hospital thing?" Kenny teased, singing the theme music loudly and tunelessly.

Lyndz was turning pinker by the minute. "And what are you doing that's so exciting?" she snapped. "Being a boring football player – oh, thrill, thrill, I don't think!"

"Yep, you got it!" Kenny said, and jumped up. Kenny never sits still for long. "Da-da-da-DA-dada-da-da-da!" she yelled – I think it was meant to be the *Match of the Day* music – and raced around the garden like a maniac. "And McKenzie's on the ball... oh, that's a lovely move, she's taken on the Arsenal defender and she's – oh! What a goal McKenzie's scored for Leicester City! That's her hat-trick! And Leicester City wins the FA Cup!!"

She ran right round the garden, cheering and yelling, then sat down again, puffing. "How can you say that's boring? Did you see that goal I just scored? What a stonker!"

Frankie started tearing open the bags of Starmix and Flumps she'd bought along. "Back in the real world, does anyone want a sweet?" she asked.

YUM!!! Of course we did. Sweets are a staple part of our diet in the Sleepover Club. My mum would get really cross if she could see the amount of junk food we can get through – she's big on salads and healthy things which is OK, but I think sweets are much better. Mind you, I don't want to get fat or anything, so I try and hold back a bit – remember when I went on my diet? – but if you hold back too much with the Sleepover Club, you end up with no sweets at all, as they all get scoffed within five seconds.

We munched for a few minutes and then I picked up the pad of paper I'd brought out with me and tapped it on the grass. "Let's get on with it," I said.

"Yeah – 'cos we're gonna WIN!" Kenny yelled. I think she'd had too much sugar.

"I'll write," said Frankie, grabbing the paper off me. She likes to write everything just 'cos she's the only one who can do joined-up writing. "The Sleepover Club hits the catwalk! I hope you've all got lots of brilliant ideas for our show!"

"Ooh, teacher," said Kenny sarcastically. "I, for one, am going to model the mighty Leicester City's footy kit."

"You do surprise me, Kenz," Frankie murmured, writing it down. "I thought you'd want to be a ballerina or something."

"Or a fairy," Lyndz said, with a giggle in her voice.

"If you're really against that idea," Kenny said loudly, pretending to ignore them, "I've got an alternative one – a mad scientist, you know with lots of fake blood all down my front."

"Sounds like you'll be more of a mad butcher," I sniffed. Honestly! What was she like? Blood on the catwalk? Not if I had anything to do with it. Per-yuke!

"Fliss, we want to win, don't we?" she said.

"Yes, exactly!" I said, raising my eyebrows at her. "The grannies don't want to see a load of yucky blood on a mad scientist-butcher! We won't get any votes for that!!"

"We have to make them laugh, though," Kenny argued.

"Yeah, laugh, not frighten them to death," Rosie said. Good. She was against the butcher idea too.

"OK, OK," Kenny said huffily. "So you don't like that idea." She went into a headstand. "I'll think of another one."

I eyed her warily. Our garden is full of really lovely flowers and shrubs because my mum and Andy both like making it look nice. I know Kenny's a good gymnast, but even she has wobbly days – and I didn't want her wobbling over into my mum's foxgloves.

"Well, I am going to go for straight modelling," I told Frankie. "So you might as well write that down."

"Cowboy, footballer, model. Hmmm. This show's a bit... *bitty* at the moment," Frankie said, frowning. "Do you know what I mean? All these little bits we're each doing – we need something to bring it all together."

Rosie nearly choked on a Flump suddenly. "I've had an idea," she said, trying to chew and talk at the same time. "We can make a sort of comedy out of it – as if Fliss is the real model in the fashion show, and the rest of us are just characters who wander in, lost, if you see what I mean."

"No, I don't," said Frankie, blunt as ever.

Rosie sat up. "Well, Frankie – your spaceship has just crash-landed from Mars, and you walk in asking if anyone knows how to mend a... a... an intergalactic engine, or something."

"A *what?*" I snorted.

"And I could walk in asking for the nearest saloon bar!" Lyndz said, jumping up excitedly. "Or I could ask if anyone's seen my horse lately!"

"Yeah, something like that," Rosie said. "And all the time, Fliss is trying to do her modelling and shoo us off the stage, 'cos we're not meant to be there."

"I could dribble my football down the catwalk, then look up, all sort of surprised, and say, 'Are you lot the Liverpool reserves then?' to the oldies," Kenny said, starting to laugh, "as if I thought I was on the training ground!"

The others were all laughing now and shouting out ideas, but I wasn't quite sure. I mean, I just wanted to do it seriously, like we were real models.

"Serious will be boring," Frankie told me firmly. "This could be hilarious! I'm going to have to practise my space language. *Klinko majooliker bingbosh* – that means 'pass us those sweets'."

"There's only one other problem," Rosie said, chucking the Flumps over to her. "I don't know what I'm going to be."

"Marge Simpson?" Lyndz suggested. Rosie does a wicked impression of her.

"Mrs Pickernose from the school canteen?" Kenny offered, doing a neat backward roll on the grass. "Oof, sorry, Lyndz."

"A chicken!" Frankie said. "You could do

your chicken dance, Rosie."

"No!" Rosie said hurriedly. "I don't want to be a chicken in front of two hundred people, thanks all the same!"

"Marilyn Monroe?" I suggested.

"She's dead, Fliss," Kenny said.

"Yeah, I know she is!" I replied. "But there's that blonde wig in Lyndz's dressing up box, and..."

"I could be Elvis!" Rosie said suddenly. "And I know *he's* dead too, Kenny, before you tell me, but I could walk in looking all sleepy, like I've just woken up, saying, 'Say, what year is this, then? Gee, that must've been a mighty long nap!'"

We were all in shrieks at Rosie's impression.

"Oh, you've got to do it, Rosie," Lyndz laughed. "This is going to be really funny!"

"And grannies love a bit of Elvis," Frankie groaned. "Mine does anyway – God knows why!"

"Tea's ready!" my mum suddenly called. "Come and wash your hands, girls!"

Tea-time already! I couldn't believe it.

"We've won it already, I know it," Kenny said confidently as she bounded towards the house. "Yahooooo! Wave machine, here we come!"

CHAPTER SIX

My mum likes mealtimes to be what she calls "civilised". That means saying "please" and "thank you", no talking with your mouth full, no leaning over to grab anything from the other side of the table – and definitely no food-fights. All the food is nicely arranged in serving bowls and we usually have napkins to wear. She doesn't even like me and Callum bickering at the table – if we start having an argument, she'll send us upstairs. She just likes it all nice and calm – and civilised, I suppose.

I'm used to it of course, but I know the others find it hard to behave properly. Kenny especially gets all fidgety, like she's got ants in her pants, and Lyndz often has giggling fits for no reason. She says she's nervous, but I don't know why.

"So, how's your mum at the moment, Frankie?" Mum said.

Whoops! I forgot to tell you that Frankie's mum's pregnant. When Frankie found out she went absolutely berserk with excitement – and we were all pretty pleased too, if only 'cos it means Frankie won't be able to whinge about being an only child any more.

"She's fine," Frankie said, beaming proudly. "She stopped being sick every morning ages ago – oops, sorry, don't suppose you want to hear about that, do you? – and has had her first scan now."

"Does she know what it is yet?" Lyndz put in.

"Ahh, can you tell what it is yet?" Kenny said in a terrible Rolf Harris accent which set Lyndz off giggling.

Frankie gave them a warning look. "Er, no, she didn't want them to tell her. She wants it to be a surprise. Says it's the only thing that's going to get her through the birth, having a surprise at the end of it."

"Well, give her my best wishes," said Mum with a smile. "I'll have to dig out some of Callum's old baby clothes for her."

"Let's see… five months pregnant, the baby will have its heart, lungs, bones, arms and legs by now," Kenny said. "It'll still look a bit blobby, but…"

"How's the fashion-show planning going?" Mum said quickly. She's like me, a bit squeamish, and I could tell she didn't want to hear about half-formed babies while we were eating.

"Oh, brilliantly," Frankie said confidently. "It's going to be the funniest fashion show you've ever seen!"

"And that's just when Fliss wobbles over on her high heels!" Andy teased.

"No!" I said crossly, picking at a bit of salad with my fork.

"We've got Elvis and everything," Frankie said breezily.

"Bit of sport…" Kenny added.

"*And* some fashion," I put in.

"You lot are weird," Callum said. "You lot are really really weird!"

Frankie dazzled him with a smile. "Yeah," she agreed. "Good, isn't it?"

Next Thursday at Brownies, we'd just finished playing Up the River, Down the River, when Brown Owl clapped her hands.

"It's the concert a week on Saturday – in case anyone had forgotten!" she reminded us. "Now, I know some of you are keeping your acts secret, so next week I'm going to ask each group to come and rehearse in front of me in a separate room so I can see how all of you are getting on. So don't forget all your props and costumes, will you?"

There was a buzz of excitement, and everyone started mouthing secret things across the room to each other.

The M&Ms shot us smug looks and I saw

Kenny making rude signals back at them.

I felt a nervous pain in my tummy. It was really going to happen! Suddenly I felt nervous. The fashion show had been all my idea – and if it went wrong it was all going to be my fault!

"Wipe that look off your face," Kenny ordered me as we went out to meet her dad at the end of Brownies. "You look scared to death!"

"I am," I confessed.

"We've got loads of time!" Frankie said reassuringly. "This week we'll get it sussed, you'll see."

Sure enough, for the next few days, we were all madly planning our outfits and how we were going to fit everything into the show. By the time the weekend was over, we were starting to get a bit more organised. Rosie put together a sort of running order, telling us when we'd be coming in and out and giving us bits of dialogue. She's good at things like that, even if I think her jokes are a bit strange sometimes. But at least we kind of knew what we were going to do now.

Kenny was going to start the whole thing off with a bit of an introduction, welcoming everyone to the show and introducing me as the star model (I liked that bit). Then we'd blast out 'Spice Up Your Life' and I'd walk on wearing my first outfit. I was going to have five different outfits, and while I was changing into each one, the others would wander on and do their bits, like we'd talked about. We hadn't decided on the rest of the music yet – I wanted a Boyzone song but Kenny kept refusing to have anything to do with it. "I'm not prancing about to any of their soppy songs – I mean it!" she said every time I mentioned it.

We still hadn't solved the problem of the M&Ms though. Kenny kept coming up with plans to "nobble them", as she put it, but until we knew exactly what their acts were going to be, it was a bit difficult knowing what to do.

"Itching powder in Emma's leotard," Kenny'd say out of the blue. "Whoopee cushion under the gym mat. Fake dog poo in Emily's ballet shoes."

"Don't think about them now," I'd tell her. "Think about us. Think about the show!"

"We can deal with them on the day," Frankie would say.

It was all going to be so much fun!

Mum was helping me choose my outfits. We decided I'd start off wearing my new summer dress, then have a beach outfit, then a party outfit, then a casual jeans sort of outfit, then this black satiny evening dress Mum was helping me make out of one of her old slips. I was so excited I could hardly eat!

Frankie's outfit was going to be the most difficult to make, so we all agreed to help her with it on the Monday.

I like Frankie's house, even though I'm a bit scared of her mum and dad. They're so... *clever* sometimes, I just don't understand what they're on about, all these long words they say. Andy says that's because they're lawyers. He says he can't understand them either!

But Frankie's house is nice, and her bedroom is wicked – it's ginormous for starters, and she has lots of ace stuff in there, even a computer, lucky thing. Still that's 'cos she's an only child I suppose – but not for much longer!

All the others were there already when I walked into Frankie's bedroom.

"Doom, doom and more doom!" Frankie was moaning. She was hunched up over some silver glittery material and looking cross. "Stupid material! Why can't you go in the right place?"

"Duh… that's 'cos you've sewn it in the *wrong* place," Kenny was saying unhelpfully. "Oh, hi, Fliss – good, someone who can sew properly! Take that material off our Francesca before she totally ruins it!"

"Per-leeeze do!" Frankie said, holding it out to me. "Fliss, you're like a guardian angel walking in just at this minute!"

"Can guardian angels sew?" Rosie said doubtfully without looking up. She was glueing scrunched up bits of silver paper and the coloured cellophane from Quality Street wrappers on to a belt.

"This one can," Frankie said hopefully, still

stretching her arm out. "Can she?"

I took it from her and plopped down on the bed next to Lyndz, who was laboriously sewing blue felt stars on to the legs of Frankie's silver catsuit. Lyndz was concentrating so hard, her tongue was sticking out of the side of her mouth.

"What is it, anyway?" I asked, eyeing the tangle of silver material I was holding. I couldn't make out any shape at all.

Frankie sighed. "It was going to be a sash, to hold all my laser guns round my middle."

"Then I found this belt, which will do instead," Rosie said.

"I'm making some loops to hang things off it with pipecleaners," Kenny said. "And there's no need to turn your nose up – it's the only thing I can do. I can't sew or anything, can I?"

Course she couldn't. Kenny's fingers all turned into thumbs whenever Mrs Weaver tried to get us sewing bookmarks at school.

"The only sewing I'm going to be doing is stitching up great big wounds when I'm a doctor," she said, grinning at me. "Yum!"

"Eeurgh, gross! Shut up!" I yelled, clapping my hands to my ears. "Enough already with the gore!"

"Anyway – then I started making space gloves instead," Frankie said. "Only they're a bit difficult. And my fingers don't fit in properly now."

"Ahhh... Doctor Kenny's first operation," Kenny said. "A bit of finger shortening!"

"Thanks – but no thanks," Frankie said, sitting on her hands quickly. "Think you can fix it, Fliss? I've got to get on with my space helmet."

So *that's* what that thing on the desk was! Frankie had begged her grandad for one of his old motorbike helmets – he stuck to a car these days – and she was customising it. You guessed it – silver.

Kenny twirled a blue pipecleaner round her finger. "We could wind some of these into your hair, Frankie," she said, thoughtfully. "Make you look really funky! Funky Frankie from outta space!"

So there we all were, stitching and glueing and painting – pretty organised, wouldn't you say? Looking pretty good, wouldn't you say? That's what we thought too. But read on...

CHAPTER SEVEN

Before we knew it, it was Thursday again, and our first proper dress rehearsal in front of Brown Owl. It was dead nerve-racking, but miracle of the year, it all went pretty OK.

I did my bit first, then Kenny dribbled her football along the 'stage' area Brown Owl had chalked out on the floor. "Come on, then, you lot – are we playing or what?" she called out to an imaginary audience.

She mimed listening to an answer, then looked horrified. "What? This is the old people's home? Am I in the wrong place? Oh – sorry! Must have taken the wrong turning!"

I have to give it to her – she was good. They were going to love her!

Then it was me again, *swish swish swish*, in these long strides my mum had shown me how to do. Imagine you're gliding along the stage, she'd told me. Honestly, it's harder than it looks! But I managed to glide along without falling over – just!

Then Frankie came on and did her spaceman bit, then back to me again, then Rosie as Elvis, then me, then finally Lyndz the cowgirl. And it was really good! I was quite puffed out by all my costume changes but I think it went well.

All right, so Lyndz got the giggles when she strode past Brown Owl in her cowboy gear. Oh, and Frankie's space gun fell off her belt and went spinning off on the floor in front of her when she kicked it, but apart from that… it all seemed to go like clockwork.

Brown Owl clapped and clapped when we'd finished. "What a great idea!" she said. "I love the mixture of Felicity's modelling and you lot all coming on in character. Very funny – I think they'll really enjoy it. Well done, girls!"

We all beamed as we changed back into our Brownie uniforms and went back to the main hall.

"We were great!" Frankie said.

"We might as well pack our swimming stuff for the leisure centre tonight!" Kenny said, swaggering back down the corridor. "Girls – we've got it in the bag!"

As soon as I got back to our house after Brownies that night, though, there was pandemonium. If you've never seen my mum throwing a wobbly, think yourself lucky. It's like the Third World War going off.

The second Andy unlocked the front door, I could hear her yelling something or other.

Andy pulled a funny face at me. "Sounds like someone's in trouble," he said. "Hope it's not me."

"Or me," I added, crossing my fingers. I hadn't heard Mum this mad for ages – I'd forgotten how scary it could be.

I opened the living room door and then I

knew. It was Callum she was yelling at. And then it was my turn to scream.

I just couldn't *believe* what he'd done! The brat!

Rosie and me had spent absolutely ages making this backdrop to hang behind us for the show. It had taken us a whole afternoon to do and looked really brilliant. We'd stuck loads of big pieces of paper together and then painted on lots of stars and swirly things round the edges. Rosie had gone a bit mad with the red glitter but it still looked good. Then, in the middle, we'd painted "S.C. FASHION SUPERSTARS!" in huge red and gold letters. It looked really great, and I'd been dying to show it to the others.

Andy had promised to strengthen the back of it with some of his "mega-tape" as he calls it – you know, those huge heavy rolls of tape that stick forever – so he'd left our masterpiece in the garage.

Where it still should have been, safe and sound. Only it wasn't. It was in pieces, all over the living-room floor.

"I think you owe Felicity an apology," Mum said to Callum in her worst voice.

"What have you done?!" I yelled at him.

"We might be able to do another one..." Andy said doubtfully.

"We're doing the concert on Saturday!!!" I shouted. "We don't have *time* to do another one!"

"Sorry," Callum muttered, scuffing his feet on the carpet.

"That took us *ages*!" I raged, feeling my eyes start filling with tears at the sight of all our hard work ripped up and ruined. "Why did you have to wreck it?"

"Come on, love, don't get upset," Andy said, reaching an arm out towards me.

I was too mad to be comforted. I shook his arm off and raced upstairs. Why couldn't I have a nice brother like... like Ryan, or someone? Why did I have to live with such a pain?

Mum came upstairs after me and sat on my bed.

"Come on, wipe your face," she said,

73

passing me a tissue. "He's only a little boy and he's said he's sorry. He said he just wanted to play with it."

"Play with it? He's ripped it to bits!" I said, with a great big wobbly sob in my voice. "He's ruined it!"

"Well, fair's fair – I've told him he's got to make it up to you," Mum said, wiping my eyes. "I've told him he owes you one now – so if you can think of any way he can help you girls out with your show on Saturday, I'll make sure he does it. I know that doesn't bring back your lovely poster, but it's better than nothing, isn't it?"

"Mmm," I sniffed.

"Blow your nose, darling," Mum said. She hates anyone sniffing. "Feeling a bit better?"

"Mmm," I said. Little did she know that inside my head I was thinking, right, Callum Sidebotham! You're going to pay for this! *Big* time!

I rang the others to tell them the bad news. First Rosie, 'cos she'd been the one who'd helped make it in the first place. She's got a brother too so she kind of understood, but I could tell she felt pretty gutted about it too. "After all that work!" she sighed down the phone.

"Tell me about it," I said, sighing myself.

Frankie was more interested in Callum "owing us one", as my mum had put it. "What can we get him to do?" she said thoughtfully. I knew her brain would be going at mega-speed, trying to come up with a good way to get him back. "He could finish off my space helmet," she said after a pause. "I'm sick of trying to get it right!"

"He could play the tapes for us in the show," Kenny suggested when I asked her.

"No way," I said. "He'd put the wrong tape in or something awful. Definitely not!"

"He can be my horse," Lyndz said without a moment's hesitation when I spoke to her. "We can dress him up as a horse – how about that?"

We both burst into giggles at the thought.

"Lyndz, you're a genius," I said, "but there's

no way we can get a horse costume together in a day."

"Suppose not," she said sadly. "Let's sleep on it. I always have good ideas in my dreams!"

We met up on Friday at Kenny's for some final rehearsals and Lyndz confessed that her dreams hadn't given her any inspiration.

"I know!" Kenny said excitedly. "He can be our secret weapon against the M&Ms!"

Ooh! Somehow I'd forgotten all about them. We all sat up interestedly.

"Like how, exactly?" Frankie asked.

"Well, like – they're going to be expecting *us* to try and pull a stunt on them, aren't they?" Kenny reasoned. "Let's face it – just as much as we're expecting them to try and do the dirty on us."

"True," Rosie said. "And?"

"Well, they're not going to be watching out for Callum, are they?" Kenny went on. "So while they're trying to keep tabs on us, in walks Callum, does something to mess up their acts – and we're in the clear!"

"I don't want Callum to get in trouble," I said doubtfully. He might be a pain, but he *was* my little brother...

"What could we get him to do?" Frankie asked in a practical sort of way.

"Let's spy on the opposition," Kenny said. "That will give us some good ideas for sabotage!" She jumped up excitedly. "Come on – let's have a nosey near the M&Ms' houses – see if we can find out any of their plans!"

"Shouldn't we be rehearsing?" I asked. I wasn't sure this was such a good idea.

"Oh, the show's fine! We're brilliant!" Frankie said confidently. "I'm with Kenny on this one – let's go spying!"

So that's how we found ourselves creeping along the alley behind Sandy Lane where Emma lives, to see if we could peek into her garden.

Kenny threw herself on the ground and started crawling along, commando-style. The alley was behind all the houses so all we could see were back gardens. "We don't even know if

77

she'll be there!" I hissed to Kenny. "She might be at someone else's house, you know!"

"Let's just have a look," Kenny whispered back. "Worth a try."

As we got nearer Emma's, Kenny made us all get on our hands and knees and crawl along, in case we could be seen over the back fences. I'd put my shorts and vest top on again, but was worried about all the red dust from the alley getting on my white shorts. I was just about to stand up and say what a stupid idea I thought this was, when...

"*Ssssh!*" Frankie whispered. "Can you hear that?"

We all froze mid-crawl, and Frankie put a finger to her lips warningly. "Listen!" she whispered.

We listened.

Very faintly, we could hear the familiar (worse luck!!!) sound of Emma's voice floating on the air.

AHA!!!

"Nearer," Kenny whispered, and Frankie nodded in agreement.

We all crawled a few metres further along the alley, until Kenny grinned and pointed at the stretch of fence we were next to now. "That's it!" she mouthed.

She put an eye to a crack in the face, and pulled away hurriedly, biting a lip to stop herself laughing. "Wish I had a water pistol!" she whispered, shaking her head in disbelief. "Classic!"

Of course, we all had to have a peek, then. It was even better than we'd hoped! We'd really lucked in this time!

Instead of Emma and her stupid gymnastics group practising their routine, there was Emma and Emily both in bikinis (they were quite nice bikinis actually), sunning themselves on deckchairs, like Lady Muck and the Queen of Sheba!! And even better – both of them were discussing their acts for the show! Talk about a double whammy – this spying lark was easier than I'd thought!

CHAPTER EIGHT

"Oh, I wish we were together, Em!" Emily was saying with a dramatic sigh. "It's such a shame you're not a dancer – we could have had such fun!"

"Mmm," Emma agreed. "It's not the same, doing stuff without you. Mind you, our gymnastics display is pretty wicked, actually. There's this bit where I... Oh."

"What?"

"Well, I don't know if I should really tell you about it. It's meant to be secret, isn't it?"

"Yeah," Emily said.

Then there was this moment of silence.

They were both obviously dying to know what the other was doing – and so were we!

"Well… if you tell me what your gymnasts are doing, I'll tell you about our dance routine," Emily said after a while. "And I swear, cross my heart, I'll keep it secret."

"OK," said Emma. "And I swear, cross my heart, I'll keep yours secret, too."

There was another pause. Kenny looked as if she was about to explode with impatience. "Go on, then!" she muttered to herself. "Spill the beans, girls!"

"Well," Emily started.

Even though I could only hear her voice, I could practically see her puffing up with importance, the way she always does. Don't you just hate her?

"I've taught everyone this piece we learned at ballet school," she said. "And my ballet teacher Miss Everett has lent me all the costumes too."

Kenny pretended she was being sick in the grass and we all pulled faces at each other. I felt *sooooo* sorry for everyone else in her group having to put up with Emily bossing them all about for the last week.

"The others are all toys – Angela's a wooden soldier doll, Miko's a teddy bear, that sort of thing – and I'm a fairy who dances round, waking them all up one by one with my magic wand."

"Per-yuke!" Frankie mouthed at us. "Pass us the bucket!"

"Then we all do this dance together in our characters – you know, Angela's dancing all stiff and straight, Miko's sort of bouncy and clumsy… It's really good."

I could just picture Emily sitting back, all smug and pleased with herself. I didn't know why – it sounded awful, in my opinion.

"That sounds brilliant, Em!" Emma gushed. "I knew you'd have the star part!"

"Thanks, Em," said Emily in a pleased sort of voice. "So what are you lot doing?"

"Well, I've put together a bit of a display for the five of us," Emma started.

Emma? Organising? Surprise, surprise…

"Three of us cartwheel in from the left, two

cartwheel in from the right," she said, "and we all end up in the middle together." She paused. "Well, that's the plan, anyway, but Alana can't quite get that bit right yet."

We grinned at each other. Good old Alana Banana! She was the clumsiest thing on earth – even worse than Lyndz!

"Then I go into the splits, while the other four do forward rolls away from me, then backward rolls back into the middle again," Emma droned. "Then we each do a headstand and fold back into a crab…"

Even Kenny the mega-gymnast did a fake yawn, and we all nodded. If we were going to sit and listen to the whole of Emma's boring gymnastics routine, we'd be there all afternoon!

Frankie motioned for us to move away from the fence. "Have we got enough info, do you think?" she whispered. "I don't know how much of Emma's voice I can stand listening to, you guys!"

"We've got enough," Kenny said with a low chuckle. "Let's move!"

We were about to creep slowly off again, but then Kenny suddenly picked up some of the sandy soil that was on the ground and hurled it over the fence. "Death to the M&Ms!" she yelled, then legged it down the alley.

There were two angry yells, and then suddenly we were all charging after Kenny, laughing so hard we could hardly run properly.

"Did you see their faces?" Rosie choked. "Spitting with rage!"

"Sand all over their bare bellies!" Lyndz gasped.

"Just keep running," I pleaded. I didn't much like the thought that the M&Ms might catch us!

We piled round the corner, down Burnside Drive and back towards Kenny's house. When we were a safe distance away, we slowed to a trot.

Lyndz bent over, clutching her side. "Ow! I've got a stitch!" she moaned.

Kenny's eyes were bright. "Sorry, everyone, I couldn't resist," she said, grinning. "They were just so smug, weren't they? I can't wait to put them in their place at the show!"

We all trooped back to Kenny's house and flopped down outside in the garden again. Kenny got us all glasses of Coke and we slurped them down at once. Spying was thirsty work. My heart was racing really fast, urgh.

"What are we going to do then?" I asked. "I need to give Callum his orders, remember."

"I've got a brilliant one for Emily," Frankie said, raising one of her eyebrows (she does that a lot). "I can't imagine anything more horrible than the sight of her in a fairy costume, can you?"

"It's the worst," Lyndz agreed, slurping her Coke louder than anyone as usual.

"Well, how about if we put flour in her ballet shoes?" Frankie said with a grin. "As soon as she starts dancing about – *boof!* Flour's flying out of her shoes everywhere!"

Kenny started laughing. "Can you imagine? Clouds of flour all over the stoo-pid toys! They'll all be choking! Nice one, Frank – that's a must!"

We all agreed on that – Frankie the genius had done it again!

"How about Emma's boring gymnastics?" I asked. "The oldies will be dropping off to sleep in that one!"

"I still think whoopee cushions under the gym mats would be hilarious," Kenny said. "Just think – every time someone did a forward roll over it there would be these huge fart noises! It would be *sooooo* funny!"

Kenny demonstrated on the grass, doing massive raspberries every time she rolled over. "Whoops! Excuse me everyone!" she said.

It did look a really funny idea, even if it *was* a bit rude. The thought of Emma trying to do a serious gymnastics display with fart sounds coming from every direction just creased all of us up.

"She'd be so embarrassed!" Frankie said, giggling hysterically. "She hates things like that, doesn't she?"

"But how will we get the whoopee cushions under there in the first place?" Rosie pointed out. "We'd never get away with it!"

We all thought about that one. Hmmm. Not so easy.

"OK, let's go for itching powder in Emma's leotard," Kenny said after a while. "Simple. She looks the other way for a second and – bingo, in it goes."

"Good idea," I said. "I can't wait to see her trying to do a headstand while she's itching like crazy!"

Kenny smirked. "Blimey, I'm brilliant sometimes!" she said.

"Only sometimes," Frankie said, nudging her. "Sometimes you're just a total nutter!"

There was a scream as Kenny launched herself on top of Frankie. "Pile on!" she ordered, and we all threw ourselves on top and ended up having a massive scrap (I made sure that I was on top so I didn't get too squashed). Then Kenny dragged out the garden hose and started drenching us – so we ended up having a massive water fight. Typical Kenny – my shorts were *totally* ruined now.

So we didn't actually rehearse very much at all that day. "We'll be fine!" everyone kept saying...

But on Saturday morning when I woke up, I did not feel fine. I had terrible butterflies in my tummy. Hang on – butterflies? They were more like seagulls flapping around in there. I couldn't eat any breakfast, I felt so nervous.

"Come on, Fliss, stop picking at that toast," Andy told me. "Don't want to get the belly rumbles on the catwalk, do you?"

"How about some muesli?" Mum suggested, plonking the bag down in front of me. "That's what I always had for breakfast when I was going off on a shoot."

"Really?" I asked, reaching for the bag hesitantly. I wasn't that mad on muesli. It felt too much like eating twigs for my liking.

"Might give you the bottom burps though," Andy said and winked at me.

I snatched my hand back instantly. Forget it!

"Andy, there's no need for that!" Mum said,

sounding cross. "Ignore him, Felicity, have a bowl."

I decided that maybe I could eat my toast after all. The less I had to worry about, the better.

We'd told Mum that Callum was going to help me carry my outfits round to Frankie's house to make up for wrecking our backdrop (I didn't think she needed to know about the rest of our plans for him), so as soon as we'd finished breakfast, we set off. The show wasn't until 11.30, so we had plenty of time.

"Now, you're sure you know what you're doing?" I said on the way. "You're sure you can do it?"

"Flour in the ballet shoes, itching powder in the leotard," he said, as if he'd learned it off by heart. "And if I do it right, will Kenny let me see her pet rat again?"

I shuddered. UGH! Don't talk to me about rats! GROSS!!!!!

"I'm sure she'll let you," I said hastily. Anything to change the subject. "Look, we're nearly there now. Ask her later, eh?"

We got to Frankie's at about ten o'clock, and the others were already piling in the car. "Quick, Fliss!" Kenny yelled to me, clutching her bag of stuff. "We're all waiting for you!"

Crumbs! I started to feel a bit flustered. I hate being rushed! It made me feel nervous, with everyone charging about. And you know what happens when I feel nervous? I start feeling sick. Really, really sick!

"Are you OK, Fliss?" Rosie asked. "You look a bit green."

"I think she feels sick," Callum said importantly. "She always goes that colour. Kenny, can I see your rat later? Fliss said you might let me."

"Yeah, yeah, whatever," Kenny said. "Come on, you two, get in the car!"

It was a bit of a squash, all of us in the car. Luckily Frankie's mum and dad have got one of those big long cars with three rows of seats. Lyndz, Rosie and Kenny were already in the back seat, so Callum and I sat in the middle row. Frankie sat in the front with her dad.

We were off!

AAARGHHH!

I looked out of the window, biting my lip. I was feeling more nervous by the second…

CHAPTER NINE

It was dead hectic when we got to the old people's home. There were Brownies rushing around everywhere, with Brown Owl trying to arrange areas for everyone to get changed.

Kenny scanned the area for the M&Ms. "Aha – both targets spotted!"

I pointed them out to Callum, trying to be as subtle as possible. "*Her* ballet shoes and *her* leotard," I told him. "Got it?"

He nodded. "OK," he said seriously. Sometimes he really is an all right sort of brother, I suppose.

Brown Owl clapped her hands. "Right,

Brownies, I want to show you the stage and where you'll be coming on and going off. Can you all follow me, just for a few minutes? Then you can get on with your costumes."

"This is your chance, bro," I said to Callum. "Good luck!"

All of us Brownies trooped off after Brown Owl to check out the stage, leaving Callum all alone in the changing room to get on with the dirty work.

When Brown Owl showed us the stage, I gulped. It looked massive! It was in a big hall with absolutely loads of seats, stretching right back to the far wall. We all stood on stage together and I started feeling sicker and sicker. I mean, I'd been on stage before, in school assemblies and for the school carol concert every year – but always with loads of other people. This felt different – more like that time we did those TV commercial auditions. That was pretty terrifying, and so was this...

Lyndz squeezed my arm. "Don't worry, Fliss, you'll be great. You were brilliant at the rehearsal with Brown Owl, weren't you?"

"Was I?" I asked faintly. It seemed such a long time ago, I could hardly remember.

"You were awesome," she said warmly. Good old Lyndz. You can always count on her for a bit of moral support. And boy, did I need support!

After Brown Owl had shown us where to come on and off stage, we went back to get changed. "Fifteen minutes until the first act," she warned everyone. "Look – people are starting to sit down!"

My mouth fell open in horror as I saw a little old man shuffling forward with a walking stick. He sat right in the middle of the front row and folded his arms expectantly, a big smile on his face.

Frankie grabbed me. "Stop catching flies, Fliss," she ordered. "Let's get changed, eh?"

"Think Kate Moss!" Rosie told me. "Think glamour, think fashion!"

I pulled on my first outfit with shaking fingers. Forget fashion, all I could think about was wanting to go home.

"I did it," Callum whispered loudly to us. "I did it, you know! Just like you said!"

"Ssssh!" Kenny hissed. "Come on, Callum, come with me, I'm going to find a nice old granny to sit you next to. Then you can watch our brilliant show, and after that we'll go and see my rat, yeah?"

"Yeah!" he shouted excitedly. "Wicked!"

I glanced over at Emily to see if she'd got her shoes on yet. I'd told Callum just to stuff the flour into the toes of her shoes, so it wasn't too obvious when she put them on.

She saw me looking at her and smirked. "Is poor old Flossy feeling a teeny bit nervous?" she asked in a horrible gloating kind of voice. "Is that because she knows Flossy's fashion show is going to be a flippin' great flop?"

She and Emma burst into shrieks of laughter, and I held my breath as Emily pulled her shoes on. But she was laughing so hard, she didn't notice anything unusual. *Phew*!

"You'd think Beaky over there would learn to keep her nose out of other people's business, wouldn't you?" said Frankie in an extra-loud voice. "But no! Sadly not!"

Emma looked at Frankie with interest as she put on her space gear, and gave a witchy cackle. "I thought this was meant to be a fashion show!" she said loudly. "Not a freak show!"

"The only freaks around here are them," Rosie muttered, slicking her hair back in an Elvis quiff. "Ignore them – they won't be laughing for long."

I watched Emma pulling on her leotard from the corner of my eye. We'd given Callum a box of mega-strong itching powder that Lyndz had borrowed from one of her brothers. Hopefully that would wipe the smirk off her face.

I watched her wriggle a bit as she pulled it on, as if it wasn't very comfortable, and grinned to myself. Looked like it was starting to work already…

"Dancers, are you ready?" Brown Owl called. "You're on!"

Emily gathered her dancers together and marched them on to the stage. We giggled as we saw a trail of white floury footprints behind her, and little puffs of flour escaping out the top of her ballet pumps.

"Check it out!" Kenny whispered. "Go, Flour-foot, go!"

Brown Owl had told us we could watch the other acts from the wings, as long as we were quiet as mice. So the five of us gathered in a little huddle to see if our plan worked.

Their routine was just as we'd heard Emily describing. There was a wooden soldier, a teddy bear, a golden-haired doll and a jack-in-the-box, all sitting lifelessly on the stage. Then music started and Emily the fairy tripped lightly on to the stage, wand in her hand.

The flour wasn't too obvious at first, but as she went over to Angela, the wooden soldier, Emily did a few jumps, landing heavily on both feet each time. And just as Frankie had predicted, *puff!* – out came a cloud of flour each time!

We clutched each other, trying not to screech with laughter. You've never seen anything so hysterical! On the third *puff!*, the flour went all over Angela, right in her face –

and she let out this ginormous sneeze – *atchooooooo!* – that practically blew Emily off stage.

I thought I was going to wet myself laughing!

Emily couldn't understand what was happening, and she had this great big unfairy-like frown all over her face. Then she danced over to Miko, the teddy, and tapped her on the shoulder with her wand, and did the same series of jumps next to her. *Puff! Puff! Puff!* More flour spurted up in the air, all over Miko's teddy costume.

Someone laughed in the audience. A polite, trying-not-to-laugh laugh. Then another. Then, as Miko blurted out "Ugh! What's that?", a whole row of people started chuckling.

Somehow Emily and the dancers got through the dance but the audience laughed all the way through – which was certainly *not* what Emily had had in mind. *Ahhhh*, poor diddums!

The gymnasts were on next – and it would have been quite good apart from Emma grimacing all the way through, and fiddling with her leotard to try and stop herself itching. It was obvious she just couldn't concentrate on what she was doing.

"That girl looks in terrible pain," I heard someone in the audience say in a loud whisper, and you could tell it really put Emma off. She crashed down in the middle of a handstand, and ran off the stage, scratching like crazy.

"I'm so sorry – I think Mum must have used a dodgy washing powder," she said to Brown Owl, almost in tears. "I've never been so itchy in my life!"

"Never mind, dear," Brown Owl said kindly, but you could tell she was mentally scrubbing the gymnastics display off the prize list. *Result!* We all did secret thumbs-up signs to each other. Revenge was so sweet – especially revenge on the M&Ms!

CHAPTER TEN

Then it was us!

EEEEEEKKK!

Funnily enough, I'd enjoyed seeing the M&Ms suffer so much, I wasn't quite so nervous any more. In fact, I was feeling quite happy that our act was going to look so good, after those two major bodge-ups. The butterflies were back to being butterflies rather than the seagulls they'd been earlier that morning.

I took a deep breath, smoothed down my dress and tried to think Kate Moss.

"Ladies and gentlemen, we proudly present

our fashion show, starring supermodel Felicity Sidebotham!" Kenny boomed through the microphone. Then everyone started clapping. For me!!!

The music started, and I sashayed on to the stage wearing my new summer dress. Everyone clapped again, and I twirled and smiled my way the length of the stage, then sashayed back again to change into my next outfit. One down, four to go! It was easy! It was really going to be OK!

On came Kenny in full footy strip. The audience loved her and really laughed when she made out she was lost. All the men were cheering her, shouting, "Go on, you Foxes!" as she started going off. But then she got a bit ambitious and tried to do a handspring as part of her exit.

Uh-oh. One of her football boots came flying off and whizzed through the air, right into one of the old ladies' laps.

"Here it is, love!" the old lady called, holding the boot up.

"Well held!" Kenny called back. She'd gone

a bit red. "Thank you."

I was waiting to go on in my next outfit – my beach outfit – and I heard the M&Ms snorting with laughter about the football boot. As Kenny rushed off, I rushed on – in my crop top and short shorts.

"Ooh, very nice!" I heard an old man shout, and I blushed.

"Isn't she a pretty young thing?" someone else said in a loud whisper. "Looks just like my Janice when she was that age!"

I felt myself getting a bit flustered – and then… *total* nightmare! I somehow managed to wobble off my mum's platform sandals she'd lent me, and I ended up right on my bum! Aaargh!

"Fliss, are you OK?" Callum shouted from the audience. "That's my sister, you know!"

"Aahhhh!" said all the old dears. They thought he was part of the act!

Somehow I hobbled off stage, feeling a right nit. It was all starting to go wrong!

It didn't get any better. Lyndz got the giggles as she tried to say her lines and Frankie stumbled over the word "intergalactic" so it sounded more like she was saying "intergagagagalactic". Luckily she had so much space-age make-up on that you couldn't tell she was going red, and everyone loved the space language she'd invented.

The Elvis bit went really well – everyone oohed and ahhed as Rosie came on, with an Elvis song called 'Hound Dog' playing in the background – but then, just as I thought we could be home and dry, my very last bit went wrong again!

It was the evening wear outfit. My mum had made me this slinky dress out of an old silky black slip she didn't wear any more. It looked absolutely fab – dead sophisticated. But the only thing was, it was a teeny weeny bit long for me. I was being extra careful not to wobble off my high heels, but 'cos the dress was so long, I was having to kick out a little bit so I didn't tread on the hem of the dress. Honestly, it's *dead* complicated being a model, you know.

Then to top it off, Callum piped up from the

audience again. "Hey, Fliss! Look at me!" he shouted. "Over here!"

I turned my head a fraction to see him bouncing up and down in his chair and waving, and then before I knew it… *rrriiiiip!* I'd trodden on my hem and the whole front of the dress split open…

You know the most embarrassing thing that's ever happened to you? Multiply it by a billion. And then another billion. And then you'll still be miles away from how totally embarrassed I felt, showing my knickers to the whole of the old people's home. *Help!*

"Ooooh!" said someone.

"Oh dear!" said another.

"What a shame!" said someone else.

I burst into tears and charged off the stage like a maniac – don't ask me how I managed to run so fast with those heels on. All the others were waiting for me backstage.

"Oh, Fliss!" said Lyndz, giving me a hug. "What a nightmare!"

"Never mind," said Rosie consolingly. "You were brilliant apart from that."

"Hey, listen!" said Frankie, pointing in the direction of the stage. "Listen to that!"

We stood still for a minute – and heard it. A great roar of applause from the audience. Even though the fashion show had been a bit of a bodge, it sounded like they'd all *really* liked it!!!

Kenny peeked round the curtains and was spotted straightaway.

"Encore! Encore!" a few people shouted.

"What does that mean?" I sniffed, still feeling like an idiot.

"It means they want more!" Frankie said excitedly. "Come on – let's go and take our bows! They loved us!"

"I can't go out there like this!" I wailed. "Look – my skirt's split right the way up!"

"Hold it together," Rosie said. "And I'll stand a little bit in front of you. Come on – you were the star of the show!"

Me! The star of the show! Even though I was upset, it was brilliant to hear those words.

We went out there and everyone started cheering even louder as we took our bows.

Honestly, the most embarrassing day of my life was quickly turning into the best day of my life!

It was all over too soon and Brown Owl was hustling on the next act – the musicians.

"Well!" said Frankie as we came off stage. "Wasn't that ace? An encore!!"

"Did you hear our encore?" Kenny cooed to the M&Ms. "Oh no, I forgot – you two didn't get one, did you? Oops!"

The M&Ms didn't say anything. They knew our fashion show was miles better than their crummy acts, even if we *had* made a few mistakes!

"True talent always shows in the end," Frankie said. "Better luck next time – *not!!!*"

OK, maybe the old people had loved it, but our bit *had* gone totally wrong. So no prizes for guessing we didn't win the talent show. The musicians won the trip to the Oakworth leisure centre, after all that. But they didn't get an encore like us. I almost think I preferred it that way round. That encore was *sooooo* awesome! And after the show, when we were giving out cups of tea and coffee to the old people, loads of them came up to tell us that they thought ours was the best act. It was great! The M&Ms looked really fed up.

Kenny was a bit gutted about not winning the trip, but you never know – it's my birthday next month, so I might just ask my mum and Andy to take us there for a birthday treat. I kind of feel like we deserve *something* after all our hard work, don't you? I might even let Callum come too after he helped us out. You know what, I think he's all right after all. Sometimes.

Anyway – I'm going to have to dash, I'm afraid. We're going on holiday tomorrow and I still haven't packed a thing yet! There's been so many exciting things happening lately, the holiday's come around really quickly. I'm looking forward to swimming in the sea and lying on the beach for a week, but I've got to tell you – I'm reeeeeally going to miss the others. What am I going to do without them all?

Better get on with it, then. Mum's going to go mad if she puts her head in and sees I haven't even started yet.

This is Felicity Diana Sidebotham signing off for now. See you soon!

21

The Sleepover Club Goes for Goal!

Kenny joins the school five-a-side football team and manages to bore her friends stupid about it... that is, until the Sleepover Club form a team of their own! What a good excuse for a special football-themed sleepover...

Get your footy boots on and head for the pitch!

www.fireandwater.com
Visit the book lover's website

The Sleepover Club go Babysitting

Baby Morgan needs a babysitter urgently, and the Sleepover girls kindly agree to take charge. After all, what can be difficult about looking after a little baby? But things are never that simple for Frankie and friends —that's what makes life go crazy!

Pack up those nappies and toddle on over!

www.fireandwater.com
Visit the book lover's website

Order Form

To order direct from the publishers, just make a list of the titles you want and fill in the form below:

Name ....

Address ....

....

....

Send to: Dept 6, HarperCollins Publishers Ltd, Westerhill Road, Bishopbriggs, Glasgow G64 2QT.

Please enclose a cheque or postal order to the value of the cover price, plus:

UK & BFPO: Add £1.00 for the first book, and 25p per copy for each additional book ordered.

Overseas and Eire: Add £2.95 service charge. Books will be sent by surface mail but quotes for airmail despatch will be given on request.

A 24-hour telephone ordering service is available to holders of Visa, MasterCard, Amex or Switch cards on 0141- 772 2281.

Collins
An *Imprint* of HarperCollins*Publishers*